THIS BOOK
BELONGS TO:
_____

For Baby Jones, with love from Granny.
– Pippa

For Josephine

– Emily

All Sorts © Flying Eye Books 2020.

First edition published in 2020 by Flying Eye Books,
An imprint of Nobrow Ltd. 27 Westgate Street, London, E8 3RL.

Text © Pippa Goodhart 2020
Illustrations © Emily Rand 2020
Pippa Goodhart has asserted her right under the Copyright, Designs and Patents Act,
1988, to be identified as the Author of this Work. Emily Rand has asserted her right under the Copyright, Designs and Patents Act, 1988, to be identified as the Illustrator of this Work.

1 3 5 7 9 10 8 6 4 2

Published in the US by Nobrow (US) Inc.
Printed in Poland on FSC® certified paper.

ISBN: 978-1-912497-21-8
www.flyingeyebooks.com

Pippa Goodhart   Emily Rand

ALL SORTS

Flying Eye Books

London | New York

Frankie loved to sort things.

Sometimes she sorted
things by colour.

Sometimes she sorted things by shape.

Sometimes she sorted things by size.

She sorted sets of flowers.

She sorted sets of trees.

She sorted vehicles.

She even sorted animals.

That was quite hard.

Then Frankie tried
to sort people.

It was easy to see that some people belonged together.

But most people were hard to sort.

And Frankie had another problem...

Frankie drew a picture to work that out and she discovered something.

That felt a bit lonely.

Then it felt a bit exciting ...
which made Frankie want to dance.

So she asked the band.

The band played such a **whirly**-swirly-**boom**-bappa-**bing**-**bong**-**flip**-**flap**

mix of sizes and shapes and colours of music that...

...it mixed everybody up
into a happy dance.

When the music stopped, things settled back into muddled-up, funny old normal. Even though it was mixed up, Frankie realised...

Everyone and everything belongs in a muddle... and it works like that!

So now everything was sorted.